JAZZ SAX

LEVELS/GRADES 1–3

AURAL TESTS &
QUICK STUDIES

THE ASSOCIATED BOARD OF THE ROYAL SCHOOLS OF MUSIC

JAZZ SAX
AURAL TESTS & QUICK STUDIES
INTRODUCTION

Welcome to this book of practice aural tests and quick studies for jazz sax (alto and tenor) at Levels/Grades 1–3. This introduction outlines the basis of the tests and shows how they relate to typical lesson activities aimed at developing essential jazz skills. Separate introductions to the aural tests and quick studies can be found on page 5 and page 65 respectively. These explain the objectives of each test, how the tests are run and what the examiner will be looking for in the assessment.

Jazz is an aural tradition. Learning the essential rhythmic and melodic materials of jazz through notation is useful, but there are subtleties of timing, articulation, dynamics and embellishment that cannot be written down. Listening to performances and memorizing phrases by ear are the only ways to really get inside the music. If what you play is to contain the inflections that make it jazz, you must learn new material both by ear and from reading notation.

All jazz musicians must be able to pick out elements of the groove, melody or harmony in the musical context, so that they can respond to these elements in their improvisation. In a band or combo, for example, questions such as 'What feel is this in?', 'How does this rhythm go?' and 'Where is the pulse?' occur all the time. Musicianship skills tested as part of Associated Board jazz exams are a fundamental part of jazz performance and improvisation – they help musicians work by ear and make informed choices about what they play.

Playing by ear is important for another reason. In jazz and other improvised music, players continually listen to others and simultaneously improvise their own part. So the ability to respond to a given phrase unprepared and to invent a lively, creative and musical result is doubly important.

JAZZ SAX
AURAL TESTS & QUICK STUDIES
INTRODUCTION

Across Levels/Grades 1–3, the aural tests involve the following:

- feeling a pulse

- clapping along with the beat

- placing notes at different points within the bar

- clapping a rhythm

- remembering melodies and rhythms

- singing echoes

- inventing responses to question-and-answer exercises

The quick study covers two core skills:

- learning a short phrase, either from notation or by ear, and then playing it back straightaway, accurately and musically

- improvising a response to that phrase

The practice tests in this book cover a variety of musical styles. They may be in swing or straight 8s, and include a range of common rhythmic grooves. As well as being preparation for the assessment, the tests can provide starting points for many other activities.

Recordings of sample tests from this book are on the CDs included with the Board's tune albums for Levels/Grades 1–3. These recordings show how the elements of each test are presented in the exam and how the candidate might answer. In this book, these recorded tests carry the symbol  .

AURAL TESTS

Developing your listening and responding skills is a fundamental and hugely satisfying part of progressing as a jazz musician. Working through these tests, and on activities that develop from them, will improve your 'inner ear' and in turn impact on all aspects of your performance.

The objectives of each test, what it involves and what the examiner will be looking for are explained below.

TEST A

This test is based on a single piece of music, played by the examiner, and has three parts. You are required to:
A1   join in by clapping the pulse
A2   clap on a particular beat of the bar
A3   clap back a rhythm heard twice

A1   Clapping the pulse

This tests your ability to count along with other musicians and to join in with them. You are required to clap the pulse of the music, joining in as soon as you can.

> The examiner is looking for:
> • a confident, prompt and accurate response

A2   Clapping on a specified beat of the bar

This tests rhythmic flexibility, by asking the player to clap at a desired point in the bar, and helps develop the ability to decide where to begin and end a phrase.

The examiner will ask you to clap on a specific beat. You will be given a count-in, to establish the pulse and feel, followed by the play-through during which you must clap on the specified beat. Try to come in clearly and confidently from the start.

> The examiner is looking for:
> • an immediate response which is accurate, confident and relaxed

A3   Clapping the rhythm of a short extract

This last section tests the skill of hearing a rhythm and being able to copy it exactly. The examiner will twice play an extract from the same passage. This will be a single-line melody, taken by the left or right hand. Listen carefully to the phrase and clap it back after the second hearing. You are advised to wait until you have heard it both times before responding.

> The examiner is looking for:
> • a steady pulse
> • accurate reproduction of the phrase given, including accents and other phrasing where appropriate
> • the ability to keep going if you make a mistake

JAZZ SAX AURAL TESTS

TEST B
Singing an echo

This tests your ability to remember and sing back a phrase within a question-and-answer format. It reveals whether a candidate can feel the pulse and length of a phrase, and can come in correctly at a given place in the bar.

The examiner will give you the chord and the starting note. You will then hear the count-in to the test and four two-bar phrases, with space between each phrase for you to sing an echo. Once it has begun, the pulse will continue evenly and without stopping, so your echo must follow each phrase in time and without a pause. This is intentionally a quick-fire test, requiring quick musical reactions. You must attempt each phrase straightaway, without hesitation.

Note that tone quality is not assessed here. You may, if you prefer, hum or whistle rather than sing.

> The examiner is looking for:
> - accurate placement of the beginning of each phrase
> - accurate reproduction of the pitch, rhythm and musical character of the phrase, at the given speed and feel
> - the ability to keep going undeterred if a phrase is missed

TEST C
Improvising answering phrases

In many ways this test is the culmination of the preceding tests. Here you must respond to four short phrases, played by the examiner, with improvised answering phrases. This tests your ability to respond immediately to a given musical stimulus. You should be able to reproduce something of the style of the given phrase within a simple yet effective improvisation.

This test can be taken either on your instrument or by singing. The examiner will count in and then play a four-bar introduction, which establishes the groove. This is followed by four two-bar melodic phrases (with accompaniment), with gaps for improvised answers between each. Once it has begun, the pulse will continue evenly and without stopping. As with the echo test described above, this test counts on quick-fire musicianship.

> The examiner is looking for:
> - a flexible and creative response to the musical 'question'
> - evidence that you have identified the given rhythmic style and tempo, and can work within it
> - musical (though not necessarily predictable) rhythmic phrasing
> - improvised answers containing jazz devices, for example:
>   reproduction of elements of the question (without copying it entirely!); leaving gaps to create rhythmic interest; use of surprise; polyrhythm; or varying stressed and unstressed notes

A1 To clap the pulse of a passage of music in 3 or 4 time played by the examiner. The examiner will commence playing the passage, and the candidate will be expected to join in as soon as possible by clapping the beat.

A2 To clap on the last beat of each bar while the passage is played again. The examiner will first state the time and count in the candidate.

A3 To clap the rhythm of a short single-line extract (marked 'X') played twice by the examiner.

Medium swing ♩ = 88 **Jazz waltz**

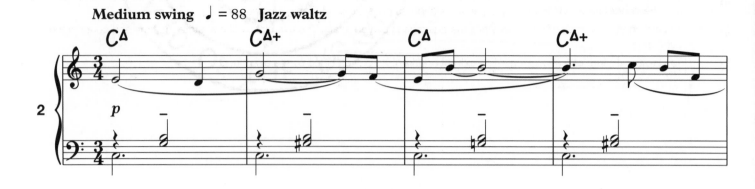

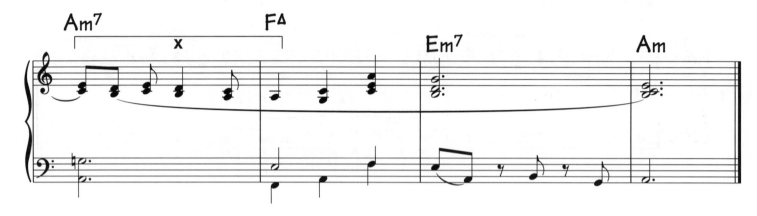

Straight 8s Latin ♩ = 96

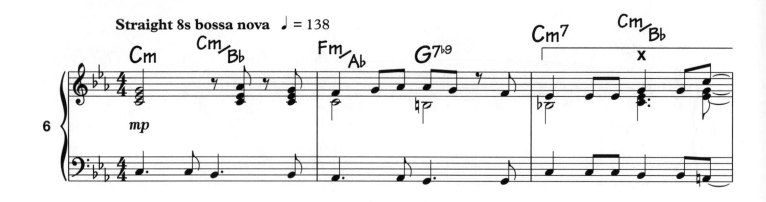

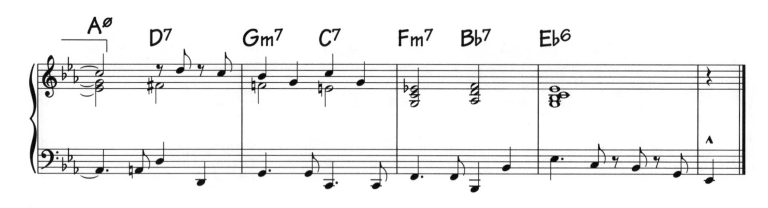

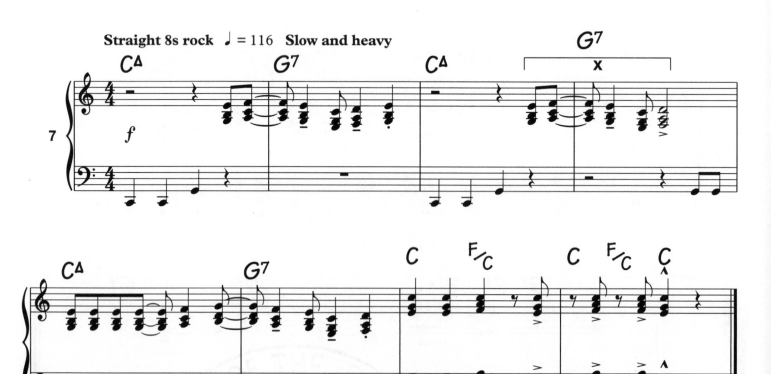

To sing, as an echo, four two-bar phrases limited to a range of a 3rd in a major or minor key or mode played by the examiner. The echoes should follow each phrase in strict time without an intervening pause. The key-chord, or chord on the root, and the starting note will first be sounded and a two-bar count-in given.

To sing or play improvised answering phrases to four two-bar phrases limited to a range of a 4th (though the answers need not be similarly limited) in a major or minor key or mode played by the examiner. The answers should follow each phrase in strict time without an intervening pause. The key-chord, or chord on the root, will first be named (in the transposed key) and sounded, and the pulse given. The examiner will then play four bars' introductory groove, before playing the first phrase to which the candidate should respond; the examiner continues with the groove throughout the test.

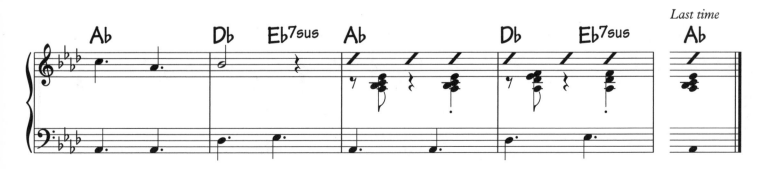

A1   To clap the pulse of a passage of music in 3 or 4 time played by the examiner. The examiner will commence playing the passage, and the candidate will be expected to join in as soon as possible by clapping the beat.

A2   To clap on the second or last beat of each bar, as directed by the examiner, while the passage is played again. The examiner will first state the time and count in the candidate.

A3   To clap the rhythm of a short single-line extract (marked 'X') played twice by the examiner.

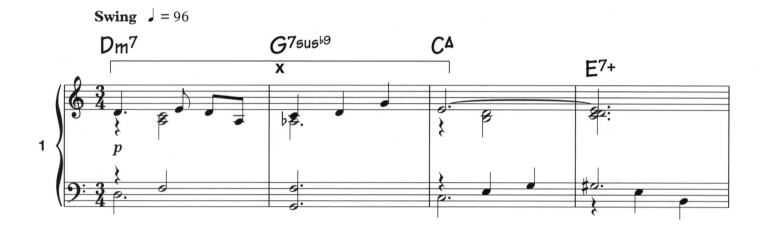

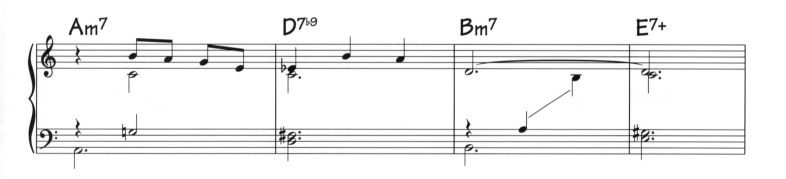

Straight 8s '60s Latin-rock ♩ = 124

Swing ♩ = 120 **Flowing jazz waltz**

To sing, as an echo, four two-bar phrases limited to a range of a 5th in a major or minor key or mode played by the examiner. The echoes should follow each phrase in strict time without an intervening pause. The key-chord, or chord on the root, and the starting note will first be sounded, and the first beat clearly indicated by the examiner, where necessary, after a two-bar count-in.

Straight 8s rock ♩ = 138

6

Straight 8s Latin ♩ = 144

7

Swing ♩ = 84

8

Straight 8s Latin ♩ = 144

9

Straight 8s rock ♩ = 112

10

To sing or play improvised answering phrases to four two-bar phrases limited to a range of a 6th (though the answers need not be similarly limited) in a major or minor key or mode played by the examiner. The answers should follow each phrase in strict time without an intervening pause. The key-chord, or chord on the root, will first be named (in the transposed key) and sounded, and the pulse given. The examiner will then play four bars' introductory groove, before playing the first phrase to which the candidate should respond; the examiner continues with the groove throughout the test.

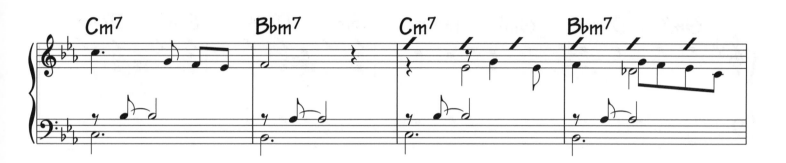

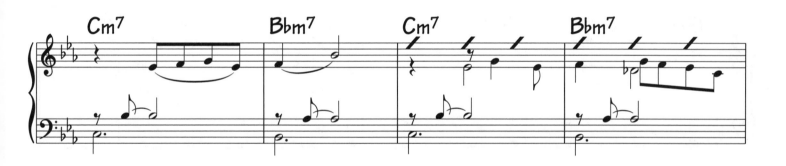

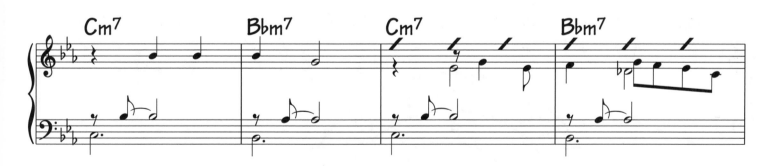

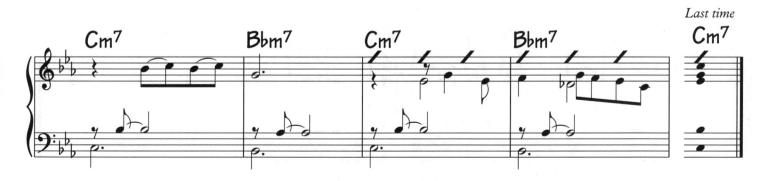

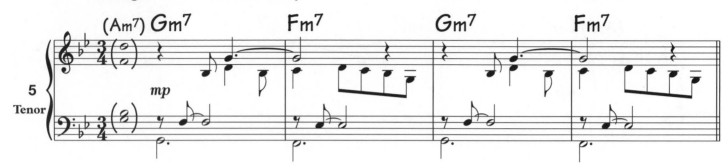

A1 To clap the pulse of a passage of music in 2, 3 or 4 time played by the examiner. The examiner will commence playing the passage, and the candidate will be expected to join in as soon as possible by clapping the beat.

A2 To clap on a set beat of each bar, chosen by the examiner, while the passage is played again. The examiner will first state the time and count in the candidate.

A3 To clap the rhythm of a short single-line extract (marked 'X') played twice by the examiner.

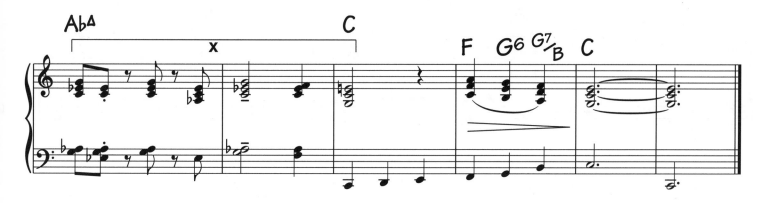

To sing, as an echo, four two-bar phrases limited to a range of a 6th in a major or minor key or mode played by the examiner. The echoes should follow each phrase in strict time without an intervening pause. The key-chord, or chord on the root, and the starting note will first be sounded, and the first beat clearly indicated by the examiner, where necessary, after a two-bar count-in.

To sing or play improvised answering phrases to four two-bar phrases in a major or minor key or mode played by the examiner. The answers should follow each phrase in strict time without an intervening pause. The key-chord, or chord on the root, will first be named (in the transposed key) and sounded, and the pulse given. The examiner will then play four bars' introductory groove, before playing the first phrase to which the candidate should respond; the examiner continues with the groove throughout the test.

QUICK STUDIES

THE TEST

In this section of the exam, the test is to play an unfamiliar passage of music, either from notation or by ear, and to improvise a response.

The test consists of two parts: a given passage (a melodic idea), which is to be played back precisely, and an improvised response in strict time without an intervening pause. For the first two Levels/Grades, the response is two bars long, the same length as the given passage. At Level/Grade 3, the passage and response are twice as long, so that the test is eight bars in total.

By ear or at sight?

You must choose to play the test at sight or by ear, though the given test will be the same either way. Ideally you should practise the tests both at sight and by ear, as both are essential jazz skills, and put your best foot forward in the exam.

Feel

Even at Level/Grade 1 the tests are in swing or straight 8s and include a range of rhythmic styles. The style given (in the playing or on the printed page) must be followed, as should the tune's tempo, which is indicated by the examiner (each written test carries a metronome mark).

The scale and the guideline pitches

You will be given the scale of the test before playing. This should form the basis of your improvisation, though you may include pitches which are outside this scale. For those reading from the page, the test has chord symbols and guideline pitches to assist you in your improvisation. If working by ear, expect the examiner to state the scale, play a chord, and sound and name the starting note of the given passage.

As your improvising skills develop you will be able to use pitches flexibly, working from three- or four-note pitch groups at Level/Grade 1 to larger, more varied pitch groups at Level/Grade 5. As a starting point, you might find it useful to improvise using only pitches included in the given passage. Those candidates working from notation may find the given chord symbols helpful. If you are working by ear, listen not to the pitches and rhythms but to the general mood and character, often defined by the speed, pulse, rhythmic style, dynamics and phrasing. Readers should also look for such signals, on the printed page.

Key signatures

At Levels/Grades 1 and 2 the key signature of the quick study follows that of the given scale – as it appears in the Associated Board's *Jazz Sax Scales*. At Level/Grade 3, where the studies are longer, a sense of key or mode emerges, and this is reflected in the key signature.

JAZZ SAX QUICK STUDIES

THE EXAM ROUTINE

First, the examiner will ask if you wish to do the test at sight or by ear.

If at sight

1. The examiner will give you the music to look at and will indicate the speed and pulse.

2. There will then be a short interval of up to half a minute in which to look through and, if you wish, try out any part of the test (before performing it for assessment).

3. At the end of the short interval, the examiner will count you in for two bars. You must play the given passage exactly as written, at the speed and feel indicated, following on from the examiner's count-in. You complete the test by improvising a response in strict time, without an intervening pause, and for the same number of bars as the given passage.

If by ear

1. While at the keyboard, the examiner will make sure you are in a position where you cannot see his/her fingers. No written notation is given to you.

2. The examiner will state the scale, play an initial chord, and name and sound the starting note (in the transposed key) of the given passage.

3. The examiner will count him/herself in for two bars and play the given passage.

4. The examiner will play the passage a second time.

5. You then have about ten seconds to try and play the passage for yourself. Note that this is unassessed, and will not be your final rehearsal.

6. The examiner will play the phrase for the third and final time, and indicate that you have another fifteen seconds or so in which to try the passage again.

7. When the fifteen seconds is up (or earlier, if you wish), the examiner will count you in. You must play the given passage exactly as heard, at the speed and feel indicated, following on from the examiner's count-in. You complete the performance by improvising a response in strict time, without an intervening pause, and for the same number of bars as the given passage.

JAZZ SAX QUICK STUDIES

Summary

At sight

Examiner: notation and speed/pulse given

Candidate: practice (up to 30 seconds)

count-in and test

By ear

Examiner: scale, chord and starting note given

Examiner: first play-through with count-in

Examiner: second play-through

Candidate: practice (up to 10 seconds)

Examiner: third play-through

Candidate: practice (up to 15 seconds)

count-in and test

WHAT THE EXAMINER IS LOOKING FOR

The following applies whether the test is completed at sight or by ear.

- accurate playing of the given passage

- a sense of performance, with the ability to keep going whatever happens. This is particularly important.

- a clear sense of pulse, and a positive yet relaxed rhythmic drive

- in the improvisation, a structured and musical response, taking into account the given passage and the scale on which it is based. The improvisation should remain broadly within the given style, and ideally be fluent, inventive and well-phrased. Credit will be given for an improvisation that sustains and builds on the main gestures and general character of the given passage.

To play *either* at sight *or* by ear, at the choice of the candidate, a two-bar passage and to improvise a two-bar continuation based on the scale indicated and used for bars 1 and 2. This scale will be any one of those set for this Level/Grade. The first two bars will be fully notated in 4/4 time and written within the range of a 4th. Chord symbols will also be provided. The chord before the start of each test is for candidates taking the test by ear; the examiner will play this first and sound and name the starting note. (When playing to 'by ear' students, transpose the following tests up a minor 3rd for alto and down a tone for tenor.)

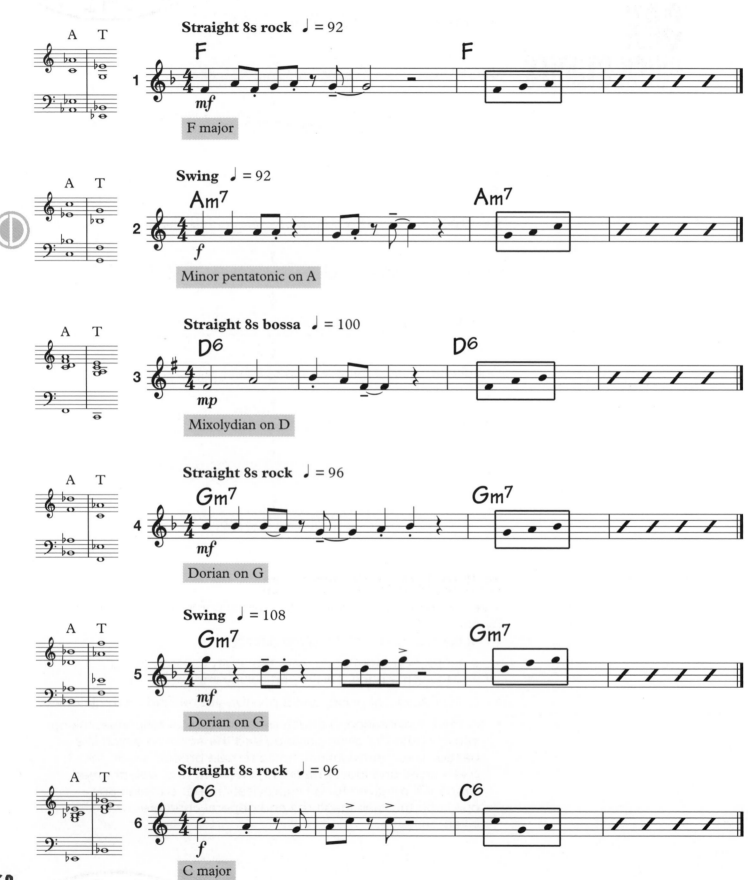

To play *either* at sight *or* by ear, at the choice of the candidate, a two-bar passage and to improvise a two-bar continuation based on the scale indicated and used for bars 1 and 2. This scale will be any one of those set up to and including this Level/Grade. The first two bars will be fully notated in 4/4 time and written within the range of a 5th. Chord symbols will also be provided. The chord before the start of each test is for candidates taking the test by ear; the examiner will play this first and sound and name the starting note. (When playing to 'by ear' students, transpose the following tests up a minor 3rd for alto and down a tone for tenor.)

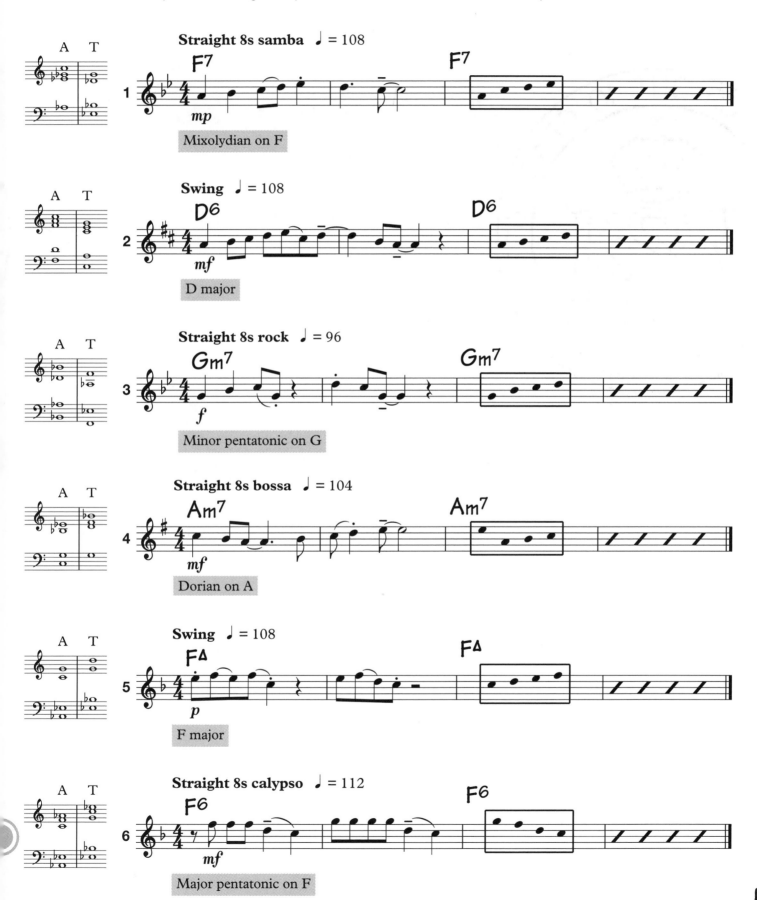

To play *either* at sight *or* by ear, at the choice of the candidate, a two-bar passage and to improvise a four-bar continuation based on the scale indicated and used for bars 1 and 2. This scale will be any one of those set up to and including this Level/Grade. The first four bars will be fully notated in 4/4 time and written within the range of a 6th. Chord symbols will also be provided. The chord before the start of each test is for candidates taking the test by ear; the examiner will play this first and sound and name the starting note. (When playing to 'by ear' students, transpose the following tests up a minor 3rd for alto and down a tone for tenor.)

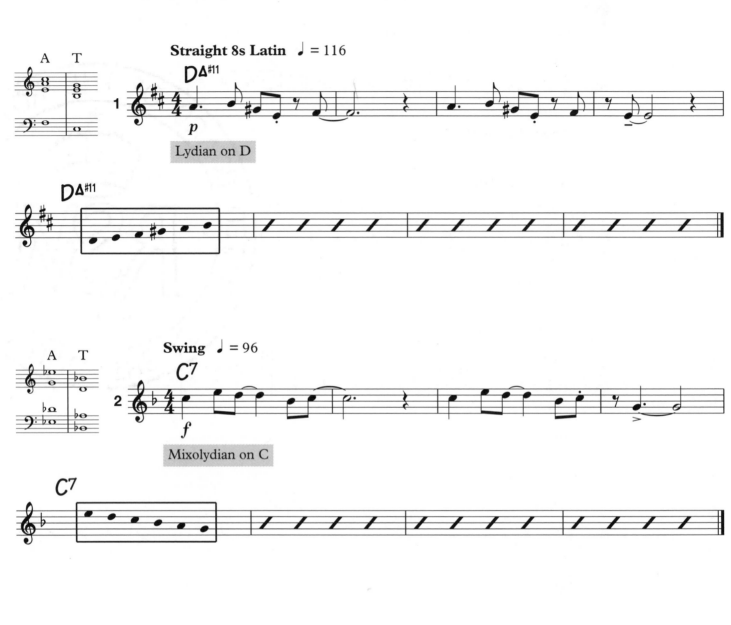

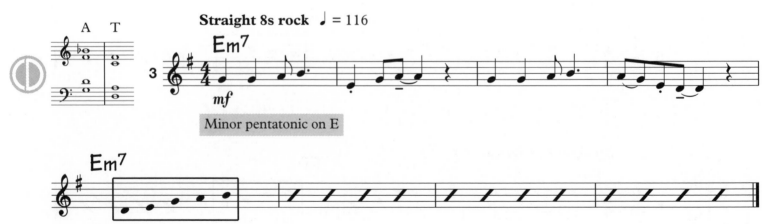

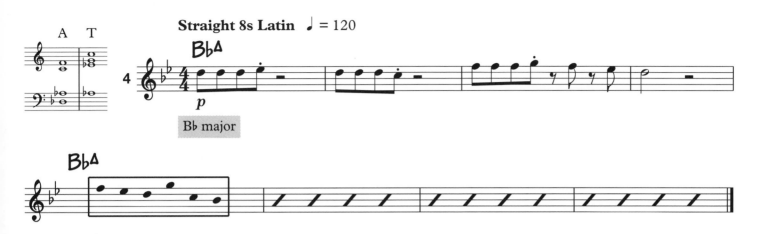

Straight 8s Latin ♩ = 120

Bb major

Swing ♩ = 112

Blues scale on A

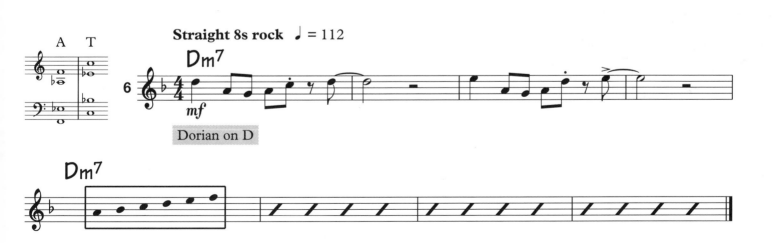

Straight 8s rock ♩ = 112

Dorian on D